Also by Sulamith Ish-Kishor

Drusilla: *A Novel of the Emperor Hadrian*
Our Eddie
The Carpet of Solomon
A Boy of Old Prague
American Promise
Magnificent Hadrian

For the great-hearted of every creed and race,
who know that we are all one.

THE MASTER OF MIRACLE

Therefore, I dwell here, and here I shall dwell until Time returns . . .

THE MASTER OF MIRACLE

A New Novel of the Golem

by Sulamith Ish-Kishor

pictures by Arnold Lobel

Harper & Row, Publishers

New York, Evanston, San Francisco, London

ACM

In warm acknowledgment to all the wonderful Harper people, especially Ursula Nordstrom, Ellen Rudin, Barbara Francis, Dorothy Hagen, Peggy Doherty—and to Arnold Lobel for the inspired sympathy of his superb drawings.

FIRST EDITION

To "Bertie,"
Mrs. Charles G. Schwartz,
one of the true "People of the Book"
in her love and service to both.

List of Illustrations

THE MASTER OF MIRACLE

At the small Pincus Synagogue in the ancient Jewish ghetto of Prague in Bohemia, up until the winter of 1847–1848, learned and important visitors sometimes would be permitted to climb the moldering staircase which led to the garret directly under the roof.

But this permission was granted only to those who knew what they were looking for, and who could be depended upon to use the gentleness and patience which would be necessary.

For here, it was said, still dwelled a man, indescribably old, still keeping watch over a great pile of charred reddish-black clay and ashes reputed to be the remains of what was once the Golem of Prague.

This aged man, crisp and thin and faded as a winter leaf, believed himself to have been born in the late 16th century in the time of the world-renowned scholar and mystic, the High Rabbi Judah Loewe, and that because of a sin which he had committed, he would not be allowed to die until the return of the Jews to Palestine and the rebuilding of Jerusalem.

Though usually dwelling in silent dream, under no change but the coming and going of light through the small arc in the domed roof, for certain persons he would become, as it were, awakened, and would to them relate a tale so fantastically mixed of known history and of legend still supported by many descendants of the High Rabbi's generation, that not even the profoundest scholar could separate actuality from whatever might lie behind those faded, mild eyes that seemed to confront with eternal patience their own destiny.

Was this pale human remnant indeed the person who had once been the boy Gideon ben Israyel, who had served the High Rabbi, and had guided the clay monster during its borrowed life? Was his story a senile reworking of a tale told by an ancestor and absorbed into his own mind as a memory rather than as a history? Was it a fantasy brought on by overstudy of the Kabalist mysteries of creation?

Or—*was it true?*

No one indeed could tell.

But there is a curious connotation.

In a winter storm of 1847–1848, the old Pincus Synagogue was struck by lightning and caught fire. In this fire the garret and everything in it was reduced to dust and swept away.

Almost exactly one hundred years later, in 1948, as we all know, the Jewish State, in abeyance since the exile in 135 A.C.E.,* was restored by vote of the United Nations, and the walls of Jerusalem were rebuilt.

Could the destiny of Gideon ben Israyel truly have been as he related it, but shortened one century by the mercy of an all-foreseeing Divinity?

The answer will only be known when the time comes for all questions to be resolved—on the Day of Judgment.

* After Christian Era.

I

When *you come to me you must come very slowly,
with quiet voices and with mild touch; you must
come like a thought or like a gentle movement of the
air.*

*For I am now as a mist or a forgetfulness, and
these pale wisps that once were human palms must not
be handled, for they have touched the seal of life which
is directly from the Creator of all.*

*Therefore, I am not of your time nor of any time,
but of the Lord's time. I am composed only of thinking and of remembering.*

For I, Gideon ben Israyel, I was once a boy in the

household of one who served the High Rabbi—yes, he, the holy Master of Miracle, Judah Loewe the Great, to whom the Eternal God confided the Secret. I, even I, have seen what only the angels of God have seen at the Beginning, the giving of life to that which had been clay.

The sin which I then committed has remained with me, and this is my punishment, decreed through him, the High Rabbi, the Lion of Judah, praised be his name, who judged that I may never relinquish life until the promise to God's chosen people be fulfilled, until Israel be restored to us, and the gates of our city Jerusalem rebuilded in glory.

Therefore, I dwell here, and here I shall dwell until Time returns, watching over this only companion, this huge shape of hallowed clay, covered as it is from human sight with many ancient relics of what once were scrolls of the Law and outworn holy books of Hebrew wisdom and prayer.

And these are companion enough for me, dwelling here alone in the sacred love of God.

Once in long whiles—I do not say time for time is not in my existence—there are sounds about me, and I see a shock of human faces and strange sorts of clothing, and I know that they look upon me as a deeply aged man who has lost what little wits he had, and they sigh and they leave me bowls containing substances upon which they believe I shall feed my body, not knowing that it no longer exists, and that I am fed by eternal light such as only the angels know.

But if you will to hear my story, if you wish to know of the Master of Miracle, and if you be of clean heart and righteous hand, cleanse then your fingers in the water basin that is at my door, and sit down, very quietly, yes, in this mold and ancient dust, and listen, and do not interrupt with questioning. For I remember. I remember well, and I remember all. What more have I to do than to remember, and tell, and wait?

2

My real father and mother I never knew, but my
father-in-God was Avrahm ben Hayim, and I would
rather be named his son than that of any other man.
For he was a disciple of the High Rabbi himself, the
Master of Miracle, the Lion of Judah, the Man of
Wisdom divine and earthly, he who was honored as
"the wonder of his time," not only throughout the
whole land of Bohemia but in the ghettoes and uni-
versities of all the world, Rabbi Judah Loewe ben*
Bezalel. And for ninety-seven years from 1512 to 1609
of the Christian era, God permitted the world the
blessing of his existence.

*Hebrew for "son of;" "baat" is "daughter of."

Avrahm ben Hayim was kind and wise, yet he did not value himself as much as one hair of the beard of the Master. And it was surely at the wish of the High Rabbi that he, who already had a grown son, took me in, regardless of my condition, when the one who first found me and saved me, she whom I called my Mutterli, passed away. She was a humble widow who had nothing to give me but her love; without her I should have died in the earliest days of my life.

The first real recollection I have—it must have been about 1572 when I was not yet two years old—is of being thrown down among a group of quickly moving big legs, while high above me rude faces roared and laughed, and something hit me sharply on the head, while a loud voice mocked, "Gentile!" At the same time, some other object came at me and lodged in my thick unkempt locks, while someone sneered, "Jew brat!" at which my Mutterli came running out, hair flying, and snatched me back into the safety of her bosom.

I was still not old enough to know which I was: gentile or Jew. As a matter of fact, I have never known, and I cannot be sure even now.

Mutterli had found me on the puddled wet cobblestones of the Judengasse, the oldest part of the Josefstadt in our old city of Prague. She often told me the whole story.

She had just lost her little boy, by cruel accident, and

still found herself waking up at night thinking she heard the baby cry; then she would realize it couldn't be, she had seen her baby dead. Finally she would fall asleep again.

But one night the crying went on and on, and though she told herself it was her imagination, she began to sense that this was real, solid crying, and the voice after all was not that of her own remembered baby. Finally she got up, threw on a shawl, and, though still bewildered, still feeling it couldn't be—how could a baby be crying in the street, and so early in the morning?— she followed the sounds out of her door, a few steps farther on to the slippery cold stones. There she saw something wriggling, wrapped in a soaked bit of cloth. She bent down and picked it up, and it *was* a baby, a real baby, a squalling, long brat, surely not even a full week old, almost naked in the early-morning rain, under the still-lighted lantern at the ghetto gate, wearing nothing but a rag torn from a woman's cheap garment.

Nobody knew how I had gotten there. My Mutterli had brought me to the local rabbi, Reb Noah, who noticed the yellow star of the Jew badge on my sole rag. He was sure it meant I was the child of Jews. But the Judengasse at that place was open and nearly opposite the slaughterhouse to which the gentile butchers brought their meat, so they used that part of the

Jew-Street almost as much as the Jews did, going in and out of the ghetto.

Reb Noah also noticed that the material was knotted firmly at the corner as if to make certain it would not fall off. Since the rag was too small to have been considered as a protection, he thought it clear that it was put on me as the only way to show my Jewish origin. It might, of course, have been done in contempt, but he thought it more likely to have been the desperate hope of a dying Jewish mother who saw no other way to tell my faith. I was too young to have been circumcised.

It was a lucky decision for me, because now she felt that God had sent to her, a childless Jewish mother, a motherless Jewish baby. So she undertook to care for me, and later received some help from the Alt-Neu Synagogue charity sisterhood, and they had me circumcised.

I should certainly know all this, for she often told me the story to make me feel sure that she had loved me as her own child from the very start. And she would add that, after she had washed me, put some of her lost boy's clothing on me, fed me, and cured me of a heavy cold, that I appeared to be rather a handsome little fellow after all, though her own child, she admitted, had been prettier, and dark, while I was fair-skinned.

By the time I was two I had grown too heavy for her to carry. I was big, sturdy, and independent, but more in the muscle than in the brain, she told me. For this reason she sometimes feared I might actually be a gentile farmworker's child. She was almost sure when she found that I didn't learn as easily as most of the Jewish boys.

But the rabbi scolded her; even Jews could sometimes be stronger in body than in brain. Look at Samson; look at Esau. Then she asked him for a name for me, and he considered, and named me Gideon, from the Bible, for Gideon had great faith and was "a mighty man of valor." And he called me Gideon ben Israyel, so now I had a whole name, and I went around all day strutting with pride and telling it to all the other boys.

Her I always called Mutterli—not quite mother, but almost. Poor Mutterli! I realized later how often she had given me the food from her own mouth, and how often I was rude and ungrateful. But she said I was good, and the only really naughty thing I ever did was once, when she had scolded me unfairly. I waited till she was out. Then I found and untied the old red kerchief in which she kept her treasures from the past, and took out the little drawing she had of her own child, and I put it on the floor and wetted on it. When it dried I put it back. Later on, I told her. That was when she dragged me to the rabbi and asked him if I was surely Jewish. He laughed and told her to take a stick to my backside. But she forgot to.

Poor Mutterli! Though we had so little, her affection made our hovel warm. Almost every Friday some housewife would have her help with the Shabbat cleaning, and she always managed to bring me home a bite of some special food; I still recall the time a family's tsimmes had burned and she got the whole of it. I thought the baked carrots and noodles in it tasted even better burnt, especially because the prunes were inside and had stayed juicy. Sometimes yellow unlaid eggs had been found inside the Shabbat chicken, and she would be given a few, hard-cooked, perhaps with a bit of gizzard or neck, with a piece of Shabbat egg-twist—a real feast!

Most often it was the butcher's wife she worked for. Mutterli brought me with her once, in the hope that I would be taken on as helper in the husband's little shop on the Judengasse. I was about seven or eight already. The woman looked at me with eyes that glittered like nails in the shadow of her headcloth; she said, what if I turned out not to be even a half-Jew, after all? I had fair hair and blue eyes—but so had many Jews, my Mutterli answered. She asked me a few questions: When does one say certain prayers; why is Shabbat a day of rest, and so on. Mutterli had taught me the answers a few days before, and I knew them, but being frightened, I stammered, and the woman shook her head darkly.

"You'll yet be sorry," she growled at Mutterli. "This is not a Jewish brain. *You* will bring him up, and *he* will join our killers." And she went inside and shut the door on us. All the way home Mutterli didn't speak to me, and then I was really scared. When we came into our little hut I asked her, "Mutterli, would you throw me away if I wasn't—" Then I saw that she was crying; she wouldn't even let me finish but hugged me close to her and said, "Never, never. I will never let them take you away from me." Then she said, "We will go to the house of the High Rabbi himself. He will know if I have done right or not." And she wiped my nose on her petticoat, then she wiped her own eyes.

Most of our neighbors felt the same way as the butcher's wife, and this seemed strange to me, because although the well-to-do ones made sure their own children were taught the Jewish faith and lore, no one seemed to care if the poor ones' kids ran wild.

But this was before the High Rabbi made the wealthy families build the Klaus School for all children, and every kind of subject was taught there.

Poor Mutterli! Though we had so little, her affection made our hovel warm.

I lived as all the other small children of the poor people lived. I carried water from the pump near the marketplace, and dawdled around the neighborhood shops and the better houses, hoping for errands, and mostly I brought home the groschen or bits of food I was given in return. With older boys—especially the bigger ones who roved with us to protect us when servants came at us with sticks—we went sifting through the ashes in the rich houses' backyards for bits of unburnt wood or for clean rushes that we could put on our own mud floors.

Sometimes I dodged what Mutterli told me to do. I couldn't see why she was always wanting me to go to old Reb Noah, to bring back his clothes for her to wash and mend, or to help him clean up his yard. He would make me stay and he would teach me the Hebrew alphabet and would want me to read big words but I didn't know what they meant. Reb Noah was a very little old man bent right over, and I was taller than he was, even when I wasn't much past eight years old. It made me sorry for him. His face was all gray beard, except his moustache was yellow under his nose, from snuff maybe. You'd never see him without his big black snuffbag—it used to be brown— except of course on Shabbat, when no one is allowed to carry anything; on Shabbat no one must do any work at all, just about breathe, and eat, and think.

Shabbat really only means "seventh day," when the Lord rested after making the world in six days. But like all Jewish holidays it begins at sunset the evening before and ends at sunset the next day. Somehow we kids were never tired on Shabbat, but we had to rest or else go to synagogue. I was glad then that I didn't have good enough clothes to go because all they did there was the men prayed in Hebrew, and I couldn't understand it.

Mutterli often cried because I couldn't go to a real school. Even at the Klaus School where the teaching was free, you had to have clothes and shoes. Then I'd feel sorry for her and I tried to learn from Reb Noah.

What I liked best was sneaking out over the Karlsbridge and sometimes down the stone stairway to the side of the river, where there was a terrace and trees and flowers that reflected in the water, and we could dive in, and swim, and sometimes catch tiny fish with our hands, but they always died before I got them home.

In springtime it was so lovely, it made you want to stay there forever, and the big boys and girls would sit on the benches or walk there. In the evening the sun made such wondrous colors around itself in the open sky, as if it were showing off to God to make Him glad He had created it.

Mostly nobody paid any attention to me and the

other youngsters; there weren't many from the ghetto, because really we weren't supposed to be out there at all. If the gentile boys called me names I fought them, so they let me alone.

But once, when I was about ten, there came a boy who was too small for me to fight, and he followed me all the way home to the gates of the ghetto, and when he saw me really going in, and felt he was safe, he shouted at me, "Christ-killer!" I didn't even turn around, but then he ran up fast behind me and spat on me. Then he darted off and around the corner, so that I couldn't even tell which way to run after him and give him a good shaking.

This made me much more angry than if he had hit me, and when I got home I asked Mutterli, who sat there weaving a hank of thread on her unsteady little handloom, in the weak flame-light of a small fire that tried to stay alive on our clay hearth.

"Mutterli, *why* do they call us names and spit on us, when we go out of the ghetto?"

She looked up and smiled at me; she was always so pleased when I came back.

"Wash your hands, Gideon; there is cheese and a heelpiece of bread." I always liked the heel and I began to grab it off the table but she stopped me. "The *hands!*"

"Other people don't wash every time they eat," I

grumbled, but I went to the little basin. "Do I have to say the blessing first, too?"

"Ach, God, while You were about it why couldn't You have sent me a child I wouldn't have to tell everything twice?" But she stroked my hair fondly as she scolded.

I said the prayer quickly and ate the bread and cheese, and then I noticed Mutterli wasn't eating. I looked at her.

"I ate already," she said, but I saw no crumbs anywhere. "What did you ask me—why they call us names? Why does it rain? Why does winter come? They call us names, they spit on us, because we're Jews, we don't have the same religion, and you shouldn't go out of the ghetto so much and you wouldn't have any trouble."

Her soft, round face looked sad and tired in the flame-light. I tried to put my little finger through one of the black curls that were always escaping under the edge of her gray marriage-wig*; she still wore it though her husband had been dead so long. She smiled at me and said, putting down her weaving,

"If you had seen me when I was young! Everyone said I was a pretty bride. . . ."

"But, Mutterli, you didn't answer me. What is a Christ-killer? Why do the other kids call us that?"

She sighed, and looked helplessly at me.

---

* Orthodox Jewish wives shave their heads and wear wigs. The idea is similar to the veil of the Muslim women.

"Who knows? It's like that everywhere in the world, not only in Prague. They call us bad names. When I was a child, thirty years ago, it was much worse. They came—oh, a wild crowd, terrible—they rushed into the ghetto—they set fire, they killed, they burned— who knows why? The Devil got hold of them! Afterward they felt sorry. Could they bring back our people who were killed for nothing?

"But then—" her face brightened—"the King—it was Maximilian who was king then—I think—or maybe already—no—yes, not Rudolf yet, it *was* Maximilian— the King himself came to our ghetto, and the Queen— oh, how beautiful she looked! with eyes like *this*—" Mutterli made two round O's with the thumbs and first fingers of her hands—"and you know what, our High Rabbi, praise to his name, he stood under a grand canopy, purple and gold, it was built right in front of the Alt-Neu Synagogue, he stood there with Rav* Meisl the rich, and Rav Kohen, and Rav Simson, and— oh, many more—I saw them all; my papa, peace be on his soul, he put me high up on his shoulder.

"And then the King and the Queen came up to the canopy—but you know what, it was a pity, they came up on foot, walking, and all dressed in black, and their fine black horses had black plumes, and they didn't wear their crowns, and their beautiful big horses walked behind them.

* Same as Mister.

16

"Papa told me it was to show their sorrow and repentance for the Jewish people that had been killed for nothing—but I was sorry they didn't wear their fine crowns and ride their fine horses. Then Papa put me down on the ground and looked very angry at me, but Mama said, 'The child is six years old! What do you want from her?'"

Mutterli's face was blooming like flowers, with a wonderful pinkness as if she were a child again.

"So all the great folks—the Christian ones that came with the King and Queen, and the Jewish ones that were under the canopy, and you know what?—they all came to each other and they talked and bowed and then they embraced each other, and after—yes, there was a great big feast for everybody, first for the great folks. There were two thrones for the King and Queen but they wouldn't sit in them, and they all went inside the synagogue, and afterward we were told they all went into the big royal castle of Hradstyn, and a big banquet was served. And you know what? It was all kosher!

"And then"—her eyes glowed—"there were fireworks all over the sky, the most beautiful fireworks—meantime they set out long wooden tables on trestles for everybody—and such a feast you will never see again. What delicious smells! The platters of hot meats, the shiny fruits, big, big cakes with all colors sweet icing—

17

and creams—and big casks of beer at the pump, free for everybody—and whole roast lambs and oxen—and it was everything kosher. There were hundreds and hundreds of Christian people from outside that came, but it was all kosher—and you know what? Lots of Christians said they wished they could have Jewish food all the time! Only some of them said where was the pork, and then a Christian priest told them, '*You* are!' Some men got up and wanted to throw out the ones that asked for pork when they knew Jews don't eat it, but the priest said, 'Never mind, they're drunk; they're pigs but they don't know it,' and everybody laughed. There was singing and joking and hugging and everyone was friends!"

Mutterli, stopping for breath, was laughing now. I laughed, too, for awhile, but then I remembered the boy that spit on me, and he didn't even know who I was.

"But, Mutterli," I asked, "what good was it? Because they're calling us names again. Maybe they're going to be bad to us again. How do we know?"

Then I was sorry I said it, because Mutterli's head bent down and her face got grown-up looking and tired as before.

"Well, we *don't* know. Who knows anything beforehand? But I heard them say at the synagogue last week there's going to be another visit here soon, not our good

King Rudolf himself, but big important people, the great Cardinal of Prague, and some of the King's wise men."

But this must have been a different kind of visit, because I don't remember any special excitement that year, the sort of thing that kids would notice and would join in. And being only ten years old or so at the time, I wouldn't be told about state affairs anyway, and maybe Mutterli wouldn't either.

3

It was not till I was almost 13 years old that Mutterli gathered the courage to go to the High Rabbi. I didn't know it then, but she had already become ill. One day, to my surprise, she called me in, washed me carefully with her own hands in spite of my protests, put a fresh shirt on me—I saw she had made it out of what had been her Shabbat dress—and even insisted on scrubbing my bare feet. Then she took out of somewhere a neat dress, almost new—and I remembered I once saw it on a lady she had worked for—she put it proudly on, and we went out together.

I asked her where we were going, but she placed

her finger on her lip and opened her dark eyes wide; so I understood it was a secret.

We came out of the very old part of the ghetto into the good streets; they were broad, with large houses that had some windows in front, and there were trees. We went past the old Community House, and the Pincus Synagogue, and the great Alt-Neu Synagogue with a broad space in front of it, and then a lot of fine houses, and then to a narrow house which looked squeezed up against a much larger one. From here you could see almost to the splendid long Karlsbridge that crossed the broad River Ultava, making blue sparkles through the trees of the rising hills among which stood the old castle of Hradstyn.

It was to the larger house that we walked.

Only, here Mutterli seemed to become afraid, and stood still on the first step, saying nothing. And then she almost turned away, as the door was opened from inside by a servant.

A lady in a fine, long blue gown was coming up to the house; she had on a large, shady hat and beside her as she turned, a young girl half-ran, half-walked, in a long pink dress; she had a shady hat, too, but she was swinging it by its pink ribbons.

The girl was so gay, with her curly brown-gold hair and wide-apart sparkling brown-gold eyes, I must have stared at her, because she kept looking at me, again and again, turning her head back and forth, and then laughing, exclaimed to the lady,

"But, Mama, look at him—he must be another cousin, though he seems so different from the others!"

She broke her hand out of her mother's and ran back down the steps to me and took hold of my arm.

"What is *your* name?" she demanded. "I am Leah baat Yitzak Kohen and this is my mama, and her name is Madame Kohen."

Her mother pulled her away, with a look at us as though she had stepped in mud.

"How old must you be, Leah, before you realize that every child who comes here is not a cousin of yours?" she rebuked her. Then to Mutterli, seeing her frightened look, she spoke rather kindly.

"What do want here, good woman?"

"What—what should a Jewish woman . . ." Mutterli stammered. "Is not this the—the house of—of—the High Rabbi, a blessing on his name?"

The lady frowned. "You have a religious question for the High Rabbi? But surely, there is a local rabbi, where you live, who can answer you? Is it a matter of kashruth?"*

"Oh, come in with us!" Leah put in promptly. "It's my grandpa you want to speak to! Come in."

"I am afraid . . ." Mutterli said, humbly.

"Afraid of *Grandpa*?" Leah laughed. "Oh, none of

* Ritual purity of food.

us are afraid of Grandpa!" She seized my hand and waved Mutterli up the steps with such a warm, inviting look, that Madame Kohen finally said,

"Oh, very well, then, come in. Leah has so very many cousins, there are always some of them coming to visit; she really doesn't know the difference."

So she took us with her, and the tall doors were opened from within, and we stood still in a narrow entrance, all draped with rich, colorful hangings, and there was a lovely smell, like lots of flowers, and like tasty food cooking.

Madame Kohen called softly, and a young man, a senior pupil at the Klaus School I think he was, with his dark robe and a small black cap on the back of his head, came out from what I noticed was really a hidden door. She said a few low words to him, and he gave my Mutterli and me a long, sharp look, then said,

"The woman's very fortunate; it happens that the High Rabbi has a few minutes now, just before prayers."

He beckoned Mutterli, and drew her through the hangings. Leah was going to follow, but Madame Kohen said, firmly,

"No, Leah, not when someone is taking a question to Grandpapa."

Madame Kohen sat down on a chair to wait. I was afraid to sit because the chairs were so fine, with yellow silk cushions placed upon them. Leah looked as if she would like to speak to me, but her mother was silent, with her head bowed; so Leah stayed still.

In a little while we heard the sound of the hangings being put back and then closed again, letting Mutterli out. I caught, within the dark shadowed chamber, a glimpse of a tall, narrow figure in white garments, a prayer shawl almost hiding his face, so that I saw only two strangely sharp eyes, a long, strong nose, and a dark curling beard that swept down his chest.

Mutterli was crying, but for joy. Tears hopped down her pale cheeks as she exclaimed,

"His blessing! The High Rabbi, praised be his name, has given me his blessing!"

Madame Kohen smiled, kindly.

"What was your question?"

"I asked, had I done right, to bring up this boy I found as a naked baby, not knowing if he was a Jew or not, only that he was within the ghetto gate, and a rag with the yellow star tied around him."

"And the High Rabbi said?"

"The High Rabbi, praised be his name, he answered me,"—she recited it like a prayer—" 'God delights in every act of mercy, for are we not all His creatures?' and he *blessed* me—our High Rabbi blessed *me*!"

The sharp wonder and delight in Mutterli's voice made me proud that I had had something to do with it. Leah suddenly kissed Mutterli, smiling happily; I'm

I caught, within the dark, shadowed chamber, a glimpse of a tall, narrow figure in white garments . . .

sure she would have kissed me, too, if she hadn't looked first at Madame Kohen, who clucked her tongue at her.

So we went home, but Mutterli was walking as proud as a queen! She stopped at the house of the butcher's wife, and boldly called her to come out, and told her the whole story, with other women listening, too; and the butcher's wife bowed her head and answered absolutely nothing and seemed ashamed to speak but went inside her house.

But next day she sent us a whole fresh-baked meat pie! And a few days after that, came a student from Madame Kohen with a woolen garment and a fringed shawl for Mutterli and a whole set of clothing for me, even a pair of good strong shoes!

After that the butcher sent for me to do small jobs in his shop, and deliver orders, and I was to take home some food every night, and four groschen every Friday.

On top of that, I was to go to the Klaus School for a year, to learn reading and writing, both Hebrew and Bohemian—arithmetic, too, if I wanted it, for Klaus School taught everything, but most of it far too high for me: geometry and physics and astronomy and the ancient tongues which the scholars and priests used when they came together.

I didn't much like going to school, but sometimes it was exciting. Once I saw a great crowd around, and I was told that the famous Swedish astronomer, Tycho

Brahe, had come to lecture there, in honor of our High Rabbi. We were all very proud of this, but not too surprised.

For to our High Rabbi, the Holy Roman Emperor himself had sent his dreams to be interpreted, and had acted according to his advice, just as Pharaoh in old Egypt had listened to the interpretations of Joseph, son of Jacob. To our High Rabbi, Judah Loewe, even the great Cardinal of Prague, Johann Sylvester, showed deference. Because of his great piety, his vast learning, his inspired wisdom, the blessing of God had descended upon Judah Loewe.

It was even whispered that our High Rabbi had performed miracles of many kinds—he was called Master of Miracle—and that through his studies and experiments with Kabala, the Book of Mystery, Zohar, the Book of Angels, and especially Yezirah, the Book of Creation, Rabbi Loewe could not only invoke the dead, but could cause them to arise again and walk the earth. This, of course, nobody had ever seen, for it was done only in utmost secrecy. At night, it was said, he had visions—Kabalistic commands from God in mystic numbers and letters which danced in fire before his eyes, and which he alone must interpret, solve, and execute. It was even sworn that he could exorcise Satan himself.

4

Poor Mutterli, she was rewarded for her goodness by a severe illness; her husband's relatives now came in at times to visit her—they were well-off and showed much disgust at her poverty—but there was little that they could do now to help her, if they had ever wanted to, and she mercifully soon passed away.

Her great comfort was that she had had the blessing of our High Rabbi, and that I was now fourteen and old enough to say the Kaddish, the sacred prayer for the dead, over her. I was never very good at study but for her sake I had learned the Kaddish. They let me say it for her at the great Alt-Neu Synagogue, but I cried so much that afterward I was doubtful if God could really have heard the words, and so I asked the Shammas, Avrahm ben Hayim, who was himself a rabbi, what he thought.

Avrahm ben Hayim looked kindly at me with his friendly dark eyes and said, "God hears the heart rather than the words." Then he said, "What will you do, now?" I just shook my head; I didn't know. So he told me to come home with him, and his wife, Elka baat Moshe, would give me dinner. He had a really rich home—or so it appeared to me then—with a great deal of furniture, and though his wife seemed at first frowning and stern, she spoke softly to me; she made me wash my hands in a water basin on a stand and then made me sit down at their own table, with a white cloth over it, and tall brass candlesticks, and so many spoons, some with little bowl-ends and some with a sort of double-spike at the end to hold food on, which was really a very clever idea of the makers.

Elka baat Moshe asked me some questions while we waited; then her husband the Shammas came in again; then I saw coming down the stairs outside the room a tallish thin figure which seemed to have a book for a head, but he descended quite easily without watching the steps, as though his feet already understood that with this young man they would have to manage by themselves. He closed the book when he came in, kissed it, and put it reverently aside on a small table-bookcase beside a wall.

"My son, Azriel," said the Shammas' wife, proudly. She nodded at me. "This is Gideon ben Israyel."

Azriel's pale face beamed on her and he kissed her cheek, and she looked very gentle just then. He and his father washed their hands at the basin, we said grace, and a great bowl of hot soup with large pieces of chicken in it was brought in by a servant. After that came a big tasty pudding of baked noodles, carrots, prunes, and spices. There was red wine and a kind of honey wine called mead, and the delicate white egg-twist bread that most people only had on Shabbat and holy days. At first my stomach felt high and closed up, but what with the company, the good and plentiful food, and the feeling that I must not waste their hospitality, I ate, though tears seemed to stay in my throat.

Azriel was already like a rabbi. He had a thin, noble face, with great dark eyes that seemed mournful but full of light; he never seemed to look at anything that was earthly. He spoke little, almost always in the Hebrew, and he was very kind, whenever he remembered anybody.

I found that a simple, clean room was prepared for me. It was once a storeroom, but there was place for a bed, and everything was clean and tidy there. It had Azriel's books in it. I saw that he treasured them and

I was very careful never to touch them. So I stayed on, and after awhile I began to help them in the ways any youngster would do, running errands, counting the candles, going with Azriel to the market or on business matters. They told me not to go to the butcher's anymore. Avrahm ben Hayim was himself a learned man and sometimes sent me to the Klaus School professors with questions not only in mystic lore but in business and finance. And after awhile they began to tell people that I was their foster-son, and Azriel's foster-brother. I was always a bit afraid of Elka baat Moshe; she was so different from my poor mixed-up, loving, helpless Mutterli. But she was reasonable and fair-minded, and though she did not regard me as a son, she treated me as a person of their household.

5

By the time I was fifteen I had had my share of fighting with youngsters of the Klaus School; anyhow I had already left it. But in the streets outside the ghetto where I would often accompany Azriel or Avrahm ben Hayim on their business with the markets or visiting the homes of non-Jewish friends, or sometimes just walking by myself, boys would start with me.

They would call me "the Christian Jew-kid" and ask me why did Moses bathe in the bulrushes and where was Esau's pot ("because Moses was a dirty Jew" and "Jacob was sitting on it") but usually I beat them up worse than they could beat me, unless there were a lot of them together.

Yes, I grew tall and strong and my strength was talked about, but it isn't true that I used to knock down four boys at one blow. It once happened that four or five older boys—they had been drinking and weren't steady on their feet anyway—wouldn't let me pass them. They stopped me, and one asked, "Hey, which way?"

I fell for it and said, "Which way to where?"

"Which way to Jerusalem?" he jeered, and they all roared with laughter.

I said, "*This* way," and I shoved him so hard into the midst of the other boys that they all fell down.

But all this was customary and nobody minded; often they'd ask me into the tavern for a mug of ale and a strudel even while they were still mopping the blood off their noses. We'd sit around and sing Bohemian songs, and if someone started any more Jew-baiting the others would knock him down and sit on his head.

Then one day there was bad news.

Times were not good; the Turkish war was on again. Money was hard to come by. Our good King Rudolf was imposing heavier taxes, and of course, friendship or no friendship, the taxes on the Jews would be double or treble the others. But also the Jews' financial advice and their foresight in economic matters were much valued by the King and his wiser ministers.

Another thing: A Spanish cargo-ship, the *Costanza,*

a great three-master of many thousand tons, carrying gold, spices, brocades, and other commissioned goods, and in which the Jewish community of Prague had a heavy investment, had failed to put in at Den Haag, and now, after forty-nine days, was feared to be missing.

There had been rough weather at sea, and it was known that the pirates of England's Queen Elizabeth were scouring the Spanish Main under command of Sir Francis Drake, not to mention the Spanish pirates who must have been on the lookout for the *Costanza* before she ever set sail. There must have been lively times on that crossing! We boys would have sold our hopes of Paradise to have been there!

Some of our investors still did not despair. The Spanish captain was an experienced man: he knew his ocean; he knew his vessel; his cannon were sound; and his men were tough seagoing rascals. But others remembered a similar catastrophe some ten or twelve years earlier: the *Santa Madre,* seventy days late, an even bigger ship than the *Costanza,* captured by pirates and wrecked, all her gold at the bottom of the sea.

When the *Costanza* proved three months late, and there came news of rejoicing at the English court, it was clear that Queen Elizabeth's pirates had captured it, probably with the help of some hired traitors on board. It was now listed as lost—captured or sunk.

Now a small group of Prague bankers, called upon to pay the heavy new taxes, besides facing the great loss of their investment in the *Costanza*, began trying to collect outstanding debts.

One of the investors was my foster-mother, Elka baat Moshe, who I now learned had brought a fortune to Avrahm ben Hayim when she married him. They decided to send Azriel, who was very keen in finance as well as in sacred matters, to call on the wealthy Count Batislav von Lehn, to ask payment of a very large sum of money which he had borrowed from them at high interest three years earlier. Some believed he had invested part of it in the *Costanza*, but others were sure he had backed the pirates, and could very well pay up. These thought he had had more than a trifle to do with the loss of the *Santa Madre* some twelve years earlier with all its Spanish gold; there had been inklings, but no one could prove it.

So Azriel set out, and I was sent to accompany him, together with two armed menservants to protect us from street-robbers or highwaymen.

It was breezy autumn weather, and we went on foot, all dressed as peasants for safety's sake. We took two days and a few hours, not counting the ferrying across water.

We came to the road that led into the estate of Count Batislav, and went on till we reached the bridge that crossed a brightly rushing little stream near the ancient castle in which he resided. A few people richly dressed were strolling on the bridge. As we entered onto the deep green lawn of the gardens, several large, strange birds with crownlike plumes strode angrily toward us on heavily feathered legs, spreading glorious fantails that shone like jeweled webs behind them. They pecked their hard beaks rudely against us until we ran, and we heard mocking laughter from the bridge. Gardeners stood about, their gardening tools in their hands, but no one showed any intention of calling off the birds.

Inside the great hall, we waited long before the servants of the Count came out to receive us.

At last we were ushered into a high chamber, fitted with tapestry hangings. There were carved wooden chairs with silken cushions, and a great desk of inlaid wood, at which sat the handsome, healthy Count, appearing to be some forty rather than fifty years of age. Behind him stood several men in everyday garments. His lordship wore a heavily furred fine robe of blue and black, and a chain richly jeweled.

Azriel bowed low, but the Count did not trouble to show him politeness.

"My good man," he asked carelessly, "what has brought you here, and why is it necessary that you enter my presence? Would not someone of my household do as well for such business as you may have?"

"My lord," said Azriel, very courteously, "perhaps these documents to which your lordship affixed your signature and seal three years ago will answer both questions."

And he held out the packet of documents. They were taken by one of the men at the Count's back. (A servant at first tried to pull them away but Azriel skilfully evaded him.)

Batislav accepted them scornfully and gave them a careless glance. Suddenly his thin, proud face turned very red. He stood up, slamming the documents onto the desk.

But he controlled himself and spoke with a pretense of good will.

"Alas, poor fellow, your masters must know that we are all pressed for gold, in these hard times. The loss of the *Costanza* has inconvenienced many."

Azriel bowed again.

"My lord, these sums were overdue even last year. This year . . ." He stopped. "Many delays have been tolerated. . . ."

Batislav laughed unpleasantly, his thin moustache curling outward. "There is much that everyone must tolerate, like it or not. Perhaps you who think you can master the world with your wealth . . . It is inconceivable to me that so small a sum as this involves . . ."

At that moment the doors opened, and a young woman, beautifully but quite simply dressed in a long green gown, appeared. She was small, dark, and graceful, with hair that shone black, dipping down her smooth white cheek. She was followed by two servants carrying silver platters with food and wine.

Batislav looked both surprised and angry.

"My dear daughter, it is not necessary for you to entertain these persons. They are mere servants."

"My lord," she answered, making him a very graceful curtsy, "I did not see them come in. I saw only that visitors had arrived, and to offer refreshment is a matter on which your lordship has chosen on many occasions to engage me."

"Well—you may take them into the next room," he said impatiently. He waved his hand toward the documents and spoke to Azriel.

"I will look these over. Perhaps something can be arranged, after you return to your employers. Do not fail to come back here, Maria-Agnes, as soon as these persons have left."

Maria-Agnes curtsied again; we bowed and went out. I then noticed that Azriel's face, which had not changed a bit under the insolence of Count Batislav, was now completely pale as he looked at Maria-Agnes.

As she poured out wine for us, I saw that she kept her large, lamplike brown eyes down, and that her cheeks had flushed dark pink, her eyelids like tiny black-fringed wings against them. She was indeed as small and delicate as a young bird; anyone could see that she and Azriel had met before, that Azriel adored her, and that she was deeply troubled by his presence.

I went out at once into the hall, wishing I had never seen them.

Azriel, who was almost ready to be ordained as a rabbi by our great Master, the High Rabbi Judah Loewe, in love with a Christian girl, and a Count's daughter at that. And the Count one of our most spiteful enemies!

It was too much. I knew I should in mere duty inform my foster-father, Avrahm ben Hayim. I also knew that I would never have the courage.

Azriel, when he came out to join me, no doubt understood this, for he did not say one word to me about her, not even to bid me be silent. And this consoled me a little, for I guessed that there was nothing actually to tell, except that he loved her.

I didn't know what Azriel told his father when we returned to Prague. But he talked with Avrahm a long time, and then both Azriel and Avrahm ben Hayim were admitted to the presence of the High Rabbi. They came away with dark and troubled looks. It was clear that deeper matters than love or money had been discussed.

And curious unpleasant things began to happen.

One day Azriel sent me to bring home a rare old Hebrew manuscript, which he had had repaired by a bookseller outside the ghetto. I noticed that people seemed to avoid me, more than was usually due to the yellow Jew-badge on my sleeve. One child pressed close to her mother, staring at me in horror, and pointing down at my feet.

I looked down, too, and saw that each step I took left a red trail, as though I had blood on my shoes! And I heard rough, mocking voices of two men passing me.

"They have met with devils at their cemetery! They must be preparing their Passover rites, when they murder a Christian to drink his blood!"

I remembered then just outside the threshold of the book-repairman, a small pot full of some red liquid had been lying overturned, and I must have stepped in it. Then I recalled a spiteful, amused look on the face of one of the young apprentices in the shop.

I thought this curious enough to recount it to Azriel. His pale face grew dark, and he asked me not to tell it to his father.

"He is troubled enough already," he added.

"Surely it was just a bit of what those young fellows call sport," I suggested.

I looked down too, and saw that each step I took left a red trail, as though I had blood on my shoes!

"Yes, we know that kind of sport too well," Azriel muttered, bitterly.

I began to think about it as we repeated the evening prayer later on, our faces turned toward the east in the direction of our ancient city of Jerusalem, a thousand miles away.

And remembering being told of other incidents that had happened to Jews walking outside the ghetto, it became clear to me, too, that hints were being given; that the old cruel lie which had caused our people so much hurt and grief—the lie that we used Christian blood for our Passover—was being revived by so-called Christian persecutors (true Christians they could not be) to hound and destroy us.

6

It was no use for me to tell myself that all was well; even a young lad like me could see that trouble was coming. The faces of Jewish men were anxious; the women scolded more; the children cried more. A spirit of evil seemed to be moving through the air in our old ghetto.

Often I saw knots of elder students talking together in low, excited voices. Noted persons were frequently seen going to or from the Klaus School or the house of the High Rabbi or the Alt-Neu Synagogue.

Sometimes they were distinguished Christians; once even, it was the great Cardinal of Prague, Johann Syl-

vester, a tall, handsome man with blond hair, fine blue
eyes, and a kindly, noble expression. He came riding a
splendidly caparisoned horse, accompanied by many
richly clad gentlemen, but he himself wore the simple
dark robe of a monk.

Everybody bowed to him as he stopped his horse and
got off at the house of the High Rabbi. Some ran to
hold his stirrup, but he would not let anyone do it. He
smiled graciously and made the sign of the cross over
us all; some Jews shrank away at that. But, after all, to
him it was the same as when our High Rabbi spread his
hands in blessing over us.

He walked quickly toward the door of the house,
which was waiting, open, for him to come in. Then the
doors were closed, and his soldiers stood in front, guard-
ing it.

After a long time, the Cardinal came out again and
rode away in the midst of his company. We understood
that he would take a secret message from the Jews to
the King.

A few days later, a Royal Proclamation was made to
a large crowd, gathered in front of the Klaus School.

An important event was to take place.

Our High Rabbi was to receive at the Alt-Neu Synagogue a deputation of Christian priests and scholars,
each day for ten days. At each of these meetings, he
would accept ten questions, in writing, handed to him

by the Great Cardinal himself, and all dealing with the question as to whether the Jews were enemies of the Christian faith and people. Then each day, after the first, the High Rabbi would himself read his own written defense of the Jews, answering the questions of the day before.

Then a Council of the Christians would decide whether the High Rabbi's rebuttals were convincing, day by day. At the end of the ten days, the Council would declare the total decision, whether the Jewish faith were judged innocent or guilty of the charges against it.

And what were these questions asking?

They were prepared, by order of the Holy Church of Christ, to inquire whether the Jewish faith demanded any actions that were harmful to Christian people; whether the Jews are required by our Law to hate or ill-treat Christians; whether the Jews were guilty in the crucifixion of Jesus; and, chiefly, whether the Jews required Christian blood to be used in their Passover ceremonials.

This last was, of course, the real question, which so frightened us. Many a time this dreadful lie had been brought up and made the chief excuse for attacks on the ghettoes at Passover time.

Some of us felt that this debate had been arranged by our good King, with the approval of the Holy

Roman Emperor and the heads of the church in other European lands, to provide an opportunity for announcing that such charges had been examined and proved to be false, and so to protect us.

Others thought the debate was planned to create an occasion for inciting mobs against us. But Avrahm and Azriel thought not; and they turned out to be right.

Although enormous crowds filled the place every time, I managed to squeeze into the Alt-Neu Synagogue on several of the days of the great debate. Since the questions were read first in ancient Hebrew and then in Latin by groups of scholars, and then answered in both languages by the High Rabbi, I naturally understood very little. But they were repeated afterward in our own language on the steps of the synagogue to the mass of people waiting outside.

The main points of the High Rabbi's answers were these:

That Jews are commanded by our Law to respect righteous people of all creeds, for all humanity will share in God's mercy; but wickedness will be punished in everyone, Jew or non-Jew.

That since, according to the Christians' own faith, Jesus was sent on earth to die for all humanity, his death was an enactment of God's will, and anyone who took part in it was unknowingly fulfilling the will of God.

And, as to the use of blood in Jewish ceremonials,

our Law forbids the use of any blood at all in our food or drink or religious rites; even the meat we eat must be washed and salted to clean off all blood (koshered) before we may eat it.

There were many more questions, but these were the most important.

For my own part, I thought it would have been wise of the Jews not to use *red* wine in our Passover rites at all, but to use white wine or ale or even water, so as not to suggest any evil charges. But I suppose this would not be thought proper by the interpreters of the Law. Somehow the easy way never seems to be the right way.

At last, after the ten days of debate, came the final day, when the envoys of the Christian church were to announce whether they believed the Jewish faith to be innocent or guilty.

I waited outside in the tense mass of Christians and Jews that day, while the final decision was made. What a roar of chattering went on among us! Then the sudden, tense silence as the gates of the Synagogue slowly opened; people began to push out of the building—you could almost see them gulping the fresh air in relief after being packed inside so long. Guards filed out and ranged in their places; nobles, gentlemen, their attendants, then the dark-robed priests, and then, at last, two tall figures.

These were the Cardinal, Johann Sylvester, this time

in crimson hat and a glory of crimson robes, his fair hair shining, his noble face uplifted to heaven, and together with him, the tall, thin, powerful figure of our High Rabbi, the white prayer shawl peaking his dark head, his face almost hidden but sending forth its own light as his arms slowly rose as if to reach up to God.

The Cardinal spoke to the hushed crowd:

"We find the Jewish faith and the Jewish people fully innocent of all these charges made against them. We do require all faithful Christians to conduct themselves accordingly, in harmony and goodwill, in peaceful and friendly dealing with all righteous persons, be they Jews or otherwise."

And, making the sign of the cross over the crowd, while our High Rabbi spread out his hands in blessing, these two stood, and shouts of joy and relief arose.

Yet I heard some harsh voices, saw some dark, angry faces and heard sneering arguments:

"And how does all this please *you?*"

"Harmony?"

"It will not last long! People forget!"

"Has the Jewish sorcerer bewitched our Cardinal? He is famous for his skill in magic!"

"Fool! Would not our Cardinal know how to protect himself?" And so on!

7

One night, early that spring, I was already asleep, when I felt someone steadily shaking my arm.

I slowly woke up. There was no light, but I recognized the voice of my foster-father, Avrahm ben Hayim, quietly calling me.

"You must be up, boy," he said. His tone, always even and kindly, this time sounded urgent and troubled.

I was young and accustomed to sleeping soundly, but even in my half-daze I knew there must be a strong reason for waking me, so I forced my eyes wide open. My unwilling feet found the floor, and I fumbled for my clothes.

"An order from the High Rabbi," was all Avrahm ben Hayim said. "Follow me quietly."

I had to hold on to his arm not to stumble in my sleepiness. We were soon out of the house, where the fresh night air brisked my eyes and mind to clearness. We were quickly joined by a third man whom I did not at first recognize—it was the night of the new moon and very dark—and from there Avrahm ben Hayim led us to the ritual bathhouse.

He unlocked the door, and to my wonder, we all three went through the long and exact ceremonials of the bath that cleansed, purified, and sanctified for the performance of sacred rites, but we had already, earlier, held the customary New Moon services.

What could this be, especially when I, ignorant and not a sanctified person such as a rabbi, Levite, or Cohen, was included?

When at last we went into the final chamber, we found there, bent in an attitude of intense prayer, dressed in long white priestly robes, his prayer shawl wound around him, the unmistakable figure of our High Rabbi.

We waited silently till he beckoned us, and then we all walked out again into the dark and quiet street. He led the way, we followed in single file. I saw that we were going toward the river, but to a point much farther out than people went for strolling. But first we

paused at the far end of the cemetery and Avrahm unlocked its rigid, clanking ancient gate. The sunken and
faded gravestones seemed to be crowding together as if
to consult each other on our strange visit. Avrahm
stooped down, and with my help lifted up a heavy
bundle, which I took and carried on my shoulders. All
I could sense about it was that it was partly heavy
metal and partly wood, wrapped around completely in
coarse cloth.

The High Rabbi was in the lead, the other man—
whom I now recognized, having seen him often though
I think I had never spoken to him—walked second. He
was Yitzak Kohen, husband of Madame Kohen, son-
in-law to the High Rabbi, and father of Leah. My
foster-father went next, and I last. We kept about seven
paces apart, to attract as little notice as possible. I
thought I saw signs that we were followed, but perhaps
these were only darker shadows.

At last we came out into open space; the river was
like a long, dark snake stretched almost silently along-
side the winding shore; a faint gleam lay on its waters
here and there. The wind was raw, but not icy.

Now the High Rabbi stopped.

He looked up, observing the sky, which was one mass
of dark, solid cloud. He began again to pray, silently.
No word, except of prayer, was uttered all this time.

Standing still, he then signaled to Yitzak Kohen with

a wide, imperious sweep of his long arm, his hand straight out, and Yitzak went and stood at a certain point. Avrahm then took his stand at the opposite point, some ten feet off from Yitzak Kohen. It was indicated to me that I was to take the fourth point, making a square.

The High Rabbi then paced, in an arc of seven steps, toward Yitzak, who made a similar quarter-circle of seven steps toward Avrahm, who then paced toward me, and I paced the fourth quarter-circle, completing it to the point where the High Rabbi had first stood.

Again the High Rabbi prayed.

When he ceased, Avrahm ben Hayim signaled me to put the bundle down and open it. I laid it down, took off the wrapping, and found a large, long, flat wooden board, and two spades. One spade Avrahm ben Hayim lifted, and began to dig up earth and to shovel it onto the board. I did the same, keeping always within the circle which our tread had marked off.

It was not light work, because the ground was almost purely clay; it was damp, sticky, and heavy. We worked what I suppose was an hour before the High Rabbi signaled us to finish. I saw that we had dug out a full circle of clay.

We then wrapped the coarse cloth around the board with its weight of clay. This time, my foster-father

The sunken and faded gravestones seemed to be crowding together as if to consult each other on our strange visit.

lifted one end, I the other, for it was now too much for one person. We paused again at the cemetery on our way back, replacing the spades, which I was glad of, for it lightened the load at least that much. Then we carried the rest into the house of the High Rabbi, and laid it down on a long table in the cellar.

Strange as the night's work was, I had felt no distress about it. I was not in the habit of questioning. But then I saw the face of the High Rabbi for a few moments in the light of a torch that somewhat strangely passed the house. The weariness, but still more the deep grief it expressed, frightened me.

As I went back with my foster-father into our house, and I felt at last allowed to speak, I whispered to him.

"My father, what is this work that we have done?"

"Do not ask, my son, it is merely a preparation. Let us pray that we may never need to use it."

"But can you not tell me what it is for?"

"We have reason to fear once more the ritual murder accusation. We may need such help as only our God can send down to us."

"But the convocation! The debate—the Cardinal's judgment—the decision of them all—"

Avrahm ben Hayim sighed. "Do you not realize that—I mean, do you think it would have been undertaken, with all its preparations, its efforts, its costs, if our good King and the noble Cardinal had not known that the enemies of goodwill were at work again?"

"But then, what has this clay to do with it?"

"As to the clay—I may not answer you."

I said no more, but I could hardly sleep, tired out though I was, for sheer wondering.

8

The narrow, dark-painted house which pressed close against the house of the High Rabbi was where Leah lived with her parents, Madame Kohen and Yitzak Kohen.

There was a green tree outside it, its roots set into a pattern of tiles bright blue and dark blue.

I was always very happy and a bit frightened to be sent there on an errand. I was always dreaming and longing that perhaps this time Leah would be there— either she would be coming out, or going in, or looking from a window, or coming down the steps into the broad place outside—and sometimes she *was* there, and

I knew how ridiculous it was that my heart should so flood with joy at the sight of her. But that is what happened. I could no more help it than a room can help lighting up when the sunshine reaches it.

It never seemed to me that I wanted anything of her, only that she should be there where I had come. When I knew that her family were in Prague, I knew that this house was joy; when I knew that the family were away, this house was gloom, bareness, and hopelessness.

Yet there was always a feeling of strangeness there, too, for actually it was a part of the house of the High Rabbi, and though it appeared that there was a solid brick wall between the two houses, some people maintained that there was a secret room between; some even said a whole set of secret rooms, one above the other, connected by narrow, turning stairs.

And while all kinds of people, dignitaries, envoys, learned men and women, servants, sometimes poor people, or those in trouble wishing to appeal to him, even children, might at various times pass through the tall front doors of the High Rabbi's house, there were said to be hidden entrances and secret ways—and some that no human ever found—of coming to him there. There were curious windows, very high up, and narrow slits in the walls. Winged snakes were seen, birds with animal bodies, and even stranger things. . . .

One of Leah's innumerable cousins, who lived in

another town and stayed with the Kohens when he attended a special course at the Klaus School, used to tell us mysterious tales! He told us that one night, when he had a stomach-ache and had to get up in the dark, somehow he came to an unknown corner and found himself going up steps. There he saw a weird thing, a quivering white thing that flashed across the place where he was, and it had eyes—and the eyes cried. So he turned round and rushed back, he didn't know where, but he did remember falling down a lot of crazy twisting steps before he got back.

But then a teacher came up to us—four or five boys we were, huddling round this boy and panting with half-fright, half-fascination at his story—and the teacher brought down on our backs and heads his round black walking stick, so that we scattered, while he screamed at us,

"Lazy idlers! For nonsense and grandma-stories they have time, but ask them to recite the first verse of Genesis, and do they know it?"

Still, I noticed that the teacher's face was pale and he had a frightened look himself.

And then one day, when I was about to deliver a message from the head of the school to the High Rabbi's front door, I turned my steps, specially to pass by Leah's house and if possible to step on the blue tiling around her tree—it felt like good luck whenever I could do that—when I happened to glance up at a tiny window at the very top of the High Rabbi's house; it was suddenly filled with a gleam of queer blue light that vanished as fast as it had come!

But then the doors at the top of the steps opened half-way and Leah came out. A servant woman was following her. All at once, it was a lovely spring afternoon again. I heard the birds singing; I saw the blossoms showing their many colors; I felt the delicious breeze—though they had all been there before, that was sure!

Her fair little face, clean and soft as a flower, was surrounded by a bright kerchief of pink and blue knotted under her plump little chin, and as she looked down the steps toward me she smiled. It was not that she was exactly beautiful, but I never saw anyone else whose whole being seemed to overflow with loving-kindness as hers did. All her movements seemed to run sparkling toward you, and you would imagine she was bringing you armfuls of fresh spring blossoms as she came.

"Peace to you, big cousin!" she greeted me.

And as usual, when I answered her I stammered first and said nothing.

"Come along, Leah baat Yitzak," said the servant harshly. Alas, so many of the boys thought they loved Leah, and the poor servant-maids were sick and tired of them and their messages and tricks and bribes and what not.

"Peace to you, Leah baat Yitzak," I said, as soon as I could, so as not to miss her greeting completely.

"He is not your cousin," the servant reminded her. And to me, "Go on, now, you; go about your business!"

They hurried off, though I heard Leah arguing with the woman all the way down the steps, "But all Israel are cousins to each other!"

Of course, she knew I was not related to her, but it would not have been surprising that Leah might think any youngster was a cousin of hers; her mother had been one of the High Rabbi's six children, and all of these had many children; one of her mother's uncles had had twenty-five, which in Kabalist reckoning was a holy number for a family. Mostly they lived in nearby towns, and all from time to time had visited Prague and stayed at the High Rabbi's house.

I handed my message to the attendant-guard who was always within the doorway there. I had to wait for an answer, and it took long, for the High Rabbi, it seemed, was not then in the house itself. I began to wonder if he were somewhere back in those mysterious chambers which we had all heard about but no one was allowed even to mention.

At last a note of reply was brought and put into my hand and I went down the steps to go back and deliver it at the Klaus School. Of course I went aside in order to pass Leah's house and to step upon the blue tiles around her tree, a ruse which had sometimes gained me the luck of another glance at her—and there, as God would have it, was Leah coming back.

This time she was not with a servant but with a boy somewhat older than herself. I knew him; he was Sheftel, a senior student, a very clever one, too, and he really was one of her cousins.

He deliberately got on the near side of Leah as they approached the house, so that he almost hid her from my line of sight.

He spoke to me.

"You, Gideon—why are you always hanging about this house? Every day that I've been here, I've seen you hanging about. What do you want, may I ask?"

"I come here when I am sent," I replied.

"Yes, that's it. You're an errand boy. You're Gideon ben nothing. You haven't even a name. So what do you expect here? Do you expect to call upon us? I am related to Leah's aunt! *My* father is rich. I'm a scholar of the first class! And you—you're—*nothing*—"

My fists began to itch. This fine, neat-faced scholar with his rosy cheeks and polished black earlocks and his embroidered skullcap. . . .

"Wait, he thinks they'll betroth him to Leah," he grinned. "Don't even dream of it, you clay lump. You won't even be looking in at the synagogue window when they give her to me in marriage. You lived in a dirty old hovel with . . ."

Leah's finger flew warningly to her lip, but too late. Something burst in me and I rushed at him; the next minute he was dodging behind the tree while I flailed at him, trying to reach him, and Leah was crying out, "No—no—Gideon! Stop! You'll kill him! For shame —stop—"

I saw that already Sheftel's face was black and blue and bleeding, though I swear I didn't know how. My own knuckles were skinned and bloody, so it must have been that I did it. And I didn't care.

But Leah had tears in her eyes. To Sheftel she cried, "Run, Sheftel! Run inside the house! What will you look like tonight at the evening meal, and *you* are to say grace! Oh, what a scandal—"

Sheftel, sniffling, gave me a murderous look, and wiped his face with her kerchief which she had snatched from her head for him, showing all her sunny hair. Then she pulled it back from his hands, and he ran, stumbling, up the steps.

Then Leah turned on me.

"Oh, Gideon ben Israyel! Look what you've done to him! And look what you did to yourself too! I was trying to make them invite you to the Sabbath meal— and now I can't! I'll wash this kerchief myself. Perhaps

I can make Sheftel tell them he—he fell. It's not really true, though; well, he fell into *your* hands! That's true. But—*you!*"

"Leah baat Yitzak, he said—"

"I heard what he said." Her anger was calming down. "He *was* very mean." Suddenly a little laugh broke past her lips. "He did look funny, dodging like that. And—Gideon—he isn't—I don't like him much."

It was as if a wing had come into my heart and was lifting it up, up, up, a million miles, beyond all the seven firmaments, beyond heaven—into the very highest . . .

"Leah—"

"I think, perhaps, it was meant for someone to—well—hit him. He is so very rich, and he is very clever, too, and his family is very ancient. They came from Spain in the exile of 1492 nearly a hundred years ago, but," and she looked for once proud and high, "not to compare with ours, for we are descended from the seed of David the King." She paused, and her face became again the darling face of Leah. "I will never marry him. I let them think so, for now. But when the time comes—"

I knew it—I knew it—

And she went on.

"When the time comes—"

And she was *not* looking at me.

My heart began its long fall—down, down, down, a million miles down, and down, but still faltering, still hovering, just a few moments more . . .

"My tutor, Saul. He lives in Wurms. He is the most wonderful person in the world and . . . a *scholar*!" She clucked her little tongue. "He could drop Sheftel and all his kind out of the left corner of his mouth. He is so good . . . and handsome as the sun!"

Her voice, her eyes, were so tender, full of dreams.

And my heart hit the blue tiles at the bottom of her tree. Yet I have loved Leah forever, and I love her still and even now, though she has for so long, so long, lain, with all whom I ever knew, at the foot of God.

That evening, my foster-mother, Elka baat Moshe, gave me stern glances, and not letting me sit down at the meal, told me, without explanation,

"You will eat for two days in the cellar."

As I went out of the room, I noticed that Avrahm ben Hayim got up from his chair and going behind her, set his hands very tenderly upon each side of her full neck, where small black curls struggled out from under her marriage-wig.

"Elka," he said softly, and there was an odd little smile on his lips, "so you never found out who it was that threw a pail of cold water over Dov when he was going in to ask you to marry him?"

She turned her head backward to look at him.

"No, I—" She stopped short.

There was such a mischievous pucker on Avrahm ben Hayim's lips, and such a comic gleam in his black eye as I never should have imagined to see in his thin, solemn face!

"Avrahmeleh! *You?*" she blurted in astonishment.

"I never had the courage to tell you," he almost whispered.

She gazed at him stupefied, then both burst into uncontrollable, almost youthful-sounding laughter.

"Oh, you scoundrel, you! I was going to say *yes* to Dov!"

"Ahah, you see? Wasn't I right?"

Elka clucked her tongue again and again.

"Elka—are you sorry?"

"Well, no. No. I always liked you better. But he was a—well, what does it matter now." She had never looked so young to me.

"And so—must Gideon eat in the cellar?"

My foster-mother came back to her usual self.

"Of course. Besides—this is different."

So I kept on down the stairs.

She was always like the laws of the Medes and the Persians. Nothing ever changed her judgments.

9

Meantime, all seemed well in our ghetto.

Passover was approaching. Now and then, some echoes of disturbance reached us from other towns: a Jewish house was set on fire at Posen, the windows of a synagogue were broken at Wurms. But afterward, as if to ensure harmony, there arrived a new deputation from the royal court, with an order proclaiming that it was forbidden to bring racial charges against the Jews; doing so would be severely punished unless the charges were proven true. Some said this order showed that new plots were being formed against us. I often wondered to myself if that mass of clay on the board had anything to do with all this, but I could not imagine what, and of course I dared not ask again.

It was not until the evening of the Great Shabbat—the Shabbat before Passover—that the trouble broke upon us.

Everyone was in the Alt-Neu Synagogue on this Shabbat, who could possibly crowd into it, for on this day the High Rabbi would deliver a special sermon. The rest of the people were in the local synagogues mostly, but a crowd waited outside the Alt-Neu, in the hope that its doors might be left open to permit a chance for them also to hear the sermon.

We were all trying to appear carefree and joyful. There was a tremendous babble and chatter from every corner. But I saw that my foster-brother Azriel was paler than usual; his head was drooping so that his earlocks fell almost to his shoulders. As for me, I was spending the waiting time trying to determine just where Leah might be placed in the curtained balcony allotted to the women, but we could only see the hangings vibrate or bulge now and then as some woman was being seated, up there to the right.

All noise abruptly ceased; the High Rabbi had entered.

The congregation rose to their feet.

In the sacred hush as he slowly mounted to the pulpit, he drew his long white prayer shawl, embroidered by pious hands with the Star of David, about his head

67

and shoulders before he opened his lips to utter the first words of the Sabbath service.

But before his voice was heard, there was a heavy clanging and clashing outside.

The doors of the synagogue were being forced open, there were loud cries of struggle and wild shouts of resistance, and then the inner doors were being pushed open against the passionate striving of the unarmed inside guards to keep them closed.

Through the doors there marched three armed strangers, and behind them a tall, impressive figure, a nobleman, by his rich robe, his curled long hair, the gems on his hat and fingers.

I recognized Count Batislav. And so, by his ghastly look, did Azriel. We stared at each other in disbelief.

Behind him, but still in the street, we caught sight of the kind of people one sees only in mobs—rootless and ragged, here and there a strong face, here and there a bitterly cruel eye, but mostly, the losers of the world, bewildered and aimless, glad of a chance to be spoken to, ready to take any side that appeals to them. We had seen such crowds as this too often not to tremble at them, for we knew what they could become, with a determined leader directing them and daggers or torches put into their hands.

In the deadly silence, Count Batislav's bootspurs clanked as he strode forward.

To our puzzlement, he stretched out his arms in a

gesture of appeal. His voice was broken, weeping, but still very loud and clear.

"Jews!" he cried out. "Hear me! I beg of you! I implore you! Have mercy on a heartbroken father! Give me back my daughter!"

All stared at him.

The High Rabbi grew pale as death.

"Give her back to me, Jews! Fellow-citizens! Fellow-humans! Hear a father's plea for his only child! Give her back to me! It cannot be too late already! Surely she has not yet been—" He shuddered as if he could not utter the word.

I saw that his eyes were not as wild as his cries; his eyes were sane, and alert, and glinting. He knew what he was doing, and with what intent.

The voice of the High Rabbi moved clear and dignified through the loud sobbing of the Count.

"Count Batislav, in the name of the living God of all, whom do you seek here?"

"My daughter—only my daughter—my poor, young, beautiful daughter! Ah, could you find no maiden less innocent, less pure—no one more fitting for the lust of your young men than my little Maria-Agnes? Where is she hidden in your ghetto? Even now, even now, if you will only give her back to me—"

Azriel had turned white as stone.

The weeping voice continued.

"She wished to become a nun, in the service of Christ!

Is this why she was chosen for—"

"Silence!"

And the dread power in the voice of the High Rabbi stilled even this man for the moment.

"We know nothing of your daughter. Leave this holy meeting-place! You will find your daughter where you yourself have placed her! Go!"

Batislav, his face now black with rage, shouted,

"Unless Maria-Agnes is returned to me, alive—" again he pretended to break down in sobs "—untouched, pure as when she was stolen from my protection, her little throat unpierced by your ritual knife—"

The Count turned, facing the mob outside who were already trying to push up toward the outer doors, "I shall appeal to these good people, these Christian mothers and fathers—"

The mob began to raise a cry of rage and sympathy.

"But not now," he called out to them, "not now, my good friends! Let us give these—these people—their chance. They have yet three days and three nights before the Passover begins. But," he turned again, "beware, Jews! You were seen one night at the cemetery with spades in your hands! Unless my Maria-Agnes is returned to me alive and unharmed, before the Passover begins, I swear that not one stone of this ghetto shall remain, not one Jew shall—"

His last words were lost in the rising noises of the

70

crowd outside, already beginning to struggle with the
mob of Batislav, and the loud cries and exclamations
of the congregation within. I caught a glimpse of Leah's
startled eyes among the crowding, frightened faces of
the women who had tugged the balcony curtains partly
open.

But Batislav marched out, and with his armed men
and a little swordplay he pushed the mob back. He had
planned something more useful to him than a mere
riot, and he was not going to let it get out of hand for
the mob's own entertainment. With some jabbing and
beating at the crowd by Batislav's spearsmen, the in-
truders were made to fall back and disperse; a few
coins glittered in the air to distract and appease some,
and to set the rest quarreling among themselves, and
then Batislav and his men mounted their horses and
rode away.

At the same time, the High Rabbi was quieting the
congregation. His deep, untroubled voice calmed and
comforted them, and he began the Holy Services as if
nothing at all had happened.

When the services were done, the people crowded
around the pulpit. As the High Rabbi prepared to leave,
he took aside three men—his son-in-law Yitzak Kohen,
father of Leah, my foster-father Avrahm, and one of
the High Rabbi's disciples, the learned Levite, Jakob
ben Hayim Sasson.

I had never seen the High Rabbi's face so stern and so determined. I heard him say to them,

"The time is here. It must be done."

"When?"

"Remain after the Sabbath."

Jakob's voice trembled.

"Must it be done? The risks—are great—"

The High Rabbi replied,

"Our danger is here, and now. We are prepared. We must act."

It was Azriel who begged me to follow the men secretly. Wringing his hands, weeping, he implored me. I was the only other person who knew of his love. He offered me all his possessions. I refused. Then he swore that he would not live, if anything happened to Maria-Agnes. He had not the slightest idea where she was. He was sure that it was because her father had found out that a Jew loved her, and that they had met, though innocently—he had not touched her—in a few secret meetings in the Count's gardens, that this plan had been worked out by our enemy.

Also, through this scheme, Azriel saw that the Count might manage to escape paying his huge debts of money to the leaders of the ghetto community. He might also obtain the sympathy of our King, instead of having to face his anger.

"But you need not worry about Maria-Agnes, Azriel," I assured him. "Even Count Batislav is not going to harm his own daughter!"

Then Azriel told me. "Maria-Agnes is not his daughter. He knows it. She knows it. But she has not dared to tell. She was saved as a small child from the wreck of the *Santa Madre*; that is all she knows. She does not know if her parents were saved. She does not know her real name. The *Santa Madre* was captured and sunk by pirates twelve years ago. She thinks Batislav had a hand in that, and also in the wreck of the *Costanza* last year. She does not know why Batislav pretends she is his daughter. But she believes that he would not hesitate to destroy her, if it suited his plans. Oh, follow them! Find out, if you can, what the High Rabbi means to do to save her. If there should be need of someone to give his life for her, *I* will do it. *I* will be the one!"

Still, I trembled to do what he asked me.

Then he begged me, by all that I owed his parents, by the years in which they had nourished and protected me, by the love of my Mutterli who had saved me without knowing if I were indeed one of her people . . .

And I promised.

10

The Great Shabbat was passed by most of the congregation in fasting and prayer, the men not leaving the synagogue until after the coming of the three stars into the firmament to show that the holy day was over.

Then the High Rabbi, followed by his son-in-law (Leah's father), by his disciple, Levite Jakob ben Hayim Sasson, and my foster-father, Avrahm ben Hayim (and me, unnoticed), went to the ritual bath.

I hid among trees, outside, in the night, until the long purification ceremonials were finished. But even though the light within there was put out at last, no one came through the door.

I realized then that the four men had gone into the tunnel which led to the house of the High Rabbi himself. This must be the mysterious quarters in the High Rabbi's own house, the part where no one else ever dared to enter unless led by the High Rabbi or his disciples.

Since some time had now passed, I judged it safe to go after them into the tunnel, by the path that bore toward the hidden side of the great house. I had pulled off my shoes, and tiptoed slowly along, listening for every sound. I began to fear that I had taken the wrong turn, but then came an echo of remote voices—yes, in a regular rhythm, a faint chanting, intense yet subdued. I followed it.

Heavy curtains hung at the door where the chanting was clearest. I lay down on the ground, lifting my head and leaning it against the damp, cool wall. Then I realized that there was no door, only hangings, and by holding back a fold of it slightly, I could see what was happening inside.

The High Rabbi was praying, with arms outstretched upward. About ten feet behind him, the other men, Avrahm, Yitzak Kohen, and Jakob Sasson were bowed in prayer. Between them, on a long table, lay a man.

No, not a man; a man-shape. A figure molded out of clay. It was not a man lying dead or unconscious, for even from where I was hiding I could see that it had never been a living thing. Neither was it a statue, for it had no pose; it merely lay flat.

Never had I seen faces so white, so strained, so pulsed with fear and ecstasy. Now the Rabbi was chanting alone, his voice rapid, tense, loud; he bowed with every word—and not a word did I understand. The language was certainly Hebrew, yet quite strange to me.

Abruptly my hands and toes, then my whole body, began to prickle and stab. My hair rose on my head; my limbs shuddered. I felt forced to stand up. I glimpsed the features of the High Rabbi, and I did not know him: his eyes were white, his face a flame from which his long beard curled down like a dark river.

The four men now began an evenly spaced procession around the clay figure, intoning mystic numbers.

Now I would have given all the rest of my life to be able to run away. But I could not move a finger. Sparks and flames were shooting through the air in separate paths; rings of light flew and trembled, brightened and vanished. From somewhere a million miles away a sound struck like vague thunder against the voices of the ecstatically crying men. And then . . .

I, too, saw it. Yes, even I, standing unbidden at the side, as the four men in regular pace moved round the huge clay body lying heavy on the table, even I, Gideon ben Israyel, saw the glory.

It came as a deepness of intense light, as if one looked into the very depths of the sun while it glowed still-white in a misted sky, light that became a Face, a Face dreadful as the bursting volcano, the earthquake, the ocean flinging itself upward in monstrous tidal waves; a Face of majestic beauty more sublime than a thousand rainbow-tinted suns—yet not a Face but a Presence. . . .

In the High Rabbi's uplifted hand there now struggled a deep blue flame. With this flame he touched the forehead of the clay creature. The flame vanished. There was a mighty crash like the splitting apart of a mountain. Then came total and utter silence and the dark.

I was trying to lift myself from the floor where I had been flung, but at first I could neither see nor hear nor feel. When slowly I stood up, and saw again, there was no longer there that huge figure of clay.

Where four men had stood, there now were five.

The fifth was of great stature, and naked. Its shaping was awkward; its slight attempts at moving an arm or leg were stiff. Yet, on the empty features, in the places under the brow where eyes were beginning to be, there lingered a reflection of the divinity which made it live. The Golem, an unfinished work of clay, was become a creature of the Eternal power.

To my terror, I heard the High Rabbi speak—to *me*! He knew—he must have known all the time—that I had stolen in! But he was not angry. He said,

"Gideon ben Israyel, your presence here gives you your task. It will be your duty to lead and to guide this Golem, whom the Eternal, blessed be His name, has granted us in our time of need.

"Respect it, for it is of God.

"Teach it, for it knows nothing of our world.

"It will know God's will. In that, follow it, and obey its guidance."

Appalled, I gazed at the Golem.

It was indeed a living being, except that nothing of it had any color but the reddish-gray tone of clay, and it was half again as big as I—and I was never small. It appeared to be a human man.

My foster-father was trembling as he put some large, heavy garments within reach of the Golem. But it made no move to clothe itself. I understood that I was to clothe it. I was able to wrap a cloak around that huge moist body. As I did this, I shook with fear lest its hands might touch me.

Nails were appearing on its finger-ends. There was now light-tinted hair on its head. The huge pallid eyes now saw me. And now, as I moved back, the colorless lips were lengthening, turning up at the ends—it was smiling at me.

A strange pain twisted my very vitals.

I had never thought that it might have feelings.

I was able to wrap a cloak around that huge moist body.

II

We had only two days left before Passover in which to find Maria-Agnes, and so far the search seemed hopeless.

The whole community was looking for her.

The physical appearance of Maria-Agnes von Lehn von Batislav was known by this time even to our dogs, for Azriel had made and tinted a drawing of her; it had been copied by all the artists and art students in the school and throughout the Josefstadt, and distributed everywhere in the ghetto. Small, graceful, with smooth dark hair, dark eyes, gentle manner, she was so much like some of our Jewish girls that we often had false reports that she was found.

Our greatest fear was lest she had actually been brought into the ghetto, where Batislav's scoundrels might later pretend to "discover" her or—God forbid it—her bleeding body, murdered by our enemies.

By the end of the second day before Passover, when it seemed almost certain that, wherever she was, at least she was not in our ghetto, I was sent for by the High Rabbi.

"Gideon ben Israyel," he commanded me, "at midnight you will descend into the deepest chamber of my house, where the Golem stands. When you enter, give it these instructions. It is to follow you—it will not be visible to any eyes but yours and Maria Agnes'—and to go through every street, every house, within this ghetto. If Maria-Agnes is here, it will find her, even if she is in the cemetery. Go, with the blessing of the Eternal."

"But, Reverend Master, how will it see—"

I was trembling with fear.

"It will see through walls and darkness."

"Reverend Master, may I not—may I not be accompanied by—by Azriel—"

The High Rabbi quelled me with a look of pure kindness.

"Did I not bid you to fear nothing?"

And, strangely, at once I felt peaceful and bold.

I found the Golem standing in the deepest cellar, where faint light entered from I knew not where.

"Golem," I said, "in the name of God, the High

Rabbi bids you to come forth. You will lead me in a final search of the ghetto for the daughter of our enemy, the Count Batislav."

To my astonishment, it lifted its huge, red-clay head, and turned it first to one side, then to the other. But it made no step forward.

Had I spoken clearly? Was it able to disobey?

I repeated the words.

Again the Golem turned its head first to one side, then to the other, then back.

There was nothing else for me to do other than to return to the High Rabbi and report this.

He was occupied with the preparation of a document, but he listened to me.

When he heard me, he frowned and was troubled.

"This means," he said, "either that Maria-Agnes is not in the ghetto—or that she is already dead. If dead, that can mean—an armed attack on Passover night."

He thought awhile.

"I have not put my orders correctly. Go back to the Golem. Bid it lead you to wherever Maria-Agnes von Lehn von Batislav is hidden, living or dead. Let it use all powers given to it. If she lives, let her be brought to the Alt-Neu Synagogue, in secret. If not, we shall then consider what is to be done."

At this moment, there was a noise in the courtyard. A servant came rushing up and almost broke into the

High Rabbi's presence. He announced that messengers had just arrived, from King Rudolf. They had ridden fast; their horses were foaming at the bit and sweating with exhaustion. They brought a command from the King that the High Rabbi present himself immediately, without loss of a moment, at the castle where the King was now residing, some fifty miles outside of Prague.

Why? What had happened? No one knew.

There was no possibility of disputing the command. Now perhaps our High Rabbi would not be with us on Passover eve, by which time, if matters had not gone well, our days would be numbered.

But we found that the King had sent a carriage, with orders that four fresh horses be harnessed to it, to assure the High Rabbi's comfort, which would seem to show that no harm was meant.

So, before our despairing eyes, he had to depart from us, in this moment of our deepest need and fear, and we had no inkling as to when he might return.

Because he did not know how long he might be absent, he trusted me with final orders in regard to the Golem:

"Gideon ben Israyel, note with care what I tell you. When Maria-Agnes is found, you must order the Golem to return to its place in the cellar. There you will utter these words: 'Golem, in the name of the Eternal Power which gave thee life, return thy spirit to whence it came. Amen.' Do not mis-speak, do not change, do not delay one syllable. The spark of life will then leave its mass, and the Golem will return to clay. You will then go out of the cellar and lock the door safely behind you."

I carefully memorized every word as he spoke and carried it away in my mind.

I went down all the inner stairway winding into the lowest chamber of the secret house.

The Golem was standing there. Obviously it could not become tired. It found it natural to stand, heavy on its two huge solid naked reddish-gray feet, never lying or sitting down. Only it seemed to me rather larger than before.

This time I was afraid in case the former shaking of its head might have been more than a denial of Maria-Agnes' presence in the ghetto. What if it meant refusal to obey? But surely the High Rabbi would have known of this possibility.

When I came toward it, and it saw me in the dim light, it smiled. I managed to smile back. Slowly it lifted a long, stiff arm, and patted my shoulder. It was like being patted by a block of stone. But I controlled any sign of pain and nodded in a friendly way as I lifted off the weight of that enormous hard hand.

"Golem," I bade it. "Help us. Conduct me to the place where Maria-Agnes von Lehn von Batislav is hidden."

At once the Golem, without a shadow of question, began to march out through the door and into the street. A crowd of our people were already gathered around the High Rabbi's house, waiting in anxiety for some sign that we were saved. For by the next evening, which would be the first night of Passover, and the celebration of the first Seder at the synagogues or in their homes, the signal must be given.

Since no one but I myself could see the Golem, it must have appeared to the people that I was walking alone, surrounded by a strange force through which no one could pass for those who were in the Golem's path were being pushed aside and thrown upon each other. Their astonishment and anger soon changed into fear, so that they ran out of the way before the Golem reached them.

We came out of the ghetto and in a short time, such great steps did the Golem take, with me running as fast as I could beside it, that soon we were out of the city itself. I dared not delay it; we had only this night and the daytime of tomorrow in which to find Maria-Agnes—and who knew how far away she might be, if living!—and to bring her back to our ghetto.

I was soon panting, out of breath. I had to stop. But the Golem, as if obeying the control of another will, abruptly turned, plucked me up in one hand as if I had been a bundle of straw, no lightweight though I was, and set me saddle-wise on its shoulders, as a father or brother sets a child.

Then it walked freely—and at what a pace!

It crossed broad roads in one step, high hills in three steps, rivers at one leap. People, who happened to be walking or riding their horses along the way, looked up and stood transfixed, not believing their eyes. Since I was visible and the Golem was not, it must have appeared to them that a young man was riding through the air some ten feet above them—and riding on nothing!

Thus we came in superhuman swiftness, to the castle of Count Batislav.

The strange jewel-tailed birds must have seen the Golem, though humans did not; perhaps all the birds and animals we had passed had seen it, for none of them had stayed in our path.

These great birds now ran at it in the moonlight, and dogs barked with deep-throated howls and crying noises. It must have seemed to any who saw them as though these richly colored creatures with their fans spread out were rushing at each other and falling dead, for some of them were left crushed and bleeding.

We came up to the broad steps and the marble terrace surrounding the front of the castle, but here the Golem turned. It walked in a direct line through hedges cut into weird dark shapes, across narrow stone paths following the outer walls, treading down flowering bushes and massive statues, leaving wreckage behind it.

It stopped at a place where the wall was rounded. It raised one long, stiff arm, and struck one blow against the heavy old wall of thick stones piled one upon the other.

The wall burst and fell apart.

The Golem set me down from its shoulders.

It walked through the opening, and I followed.

12

We were in a large, shadowy, cold cellar-chamber. At the back was the faint flare of a torch hung upon the moist brick wall. My foot struck against something heavy and wet. With horror and disgust, I saw that this was a slaughtered pig, blood oozing out of its coarse-haired body. Beside it was a stoppered stone jar and some labeled stone bottles.

On a pallet at the rear, someone who had been lying down now leapt up.

It was a slim, young being, and now I saw that it was a girl. As she ran forward, I recognized—with such a thrill of joy and thankfulness as I had never known—Maria-Agnes!

Poor little thing—she had nothing but a thin rag around her for clothing—she stared at me with terror in her eyes!

She stammered, could not utter a sound—though I saw her lips struggling to speak. I caught her in my arms as she fell in running toward me; I took her hand and kissed it, to encourage her.

"Azriel—is Azriel with you?" she gasped.

"We will bring you to him," I promised.

Her face suddenly relaxed and lightened.

"I remember you!" she exulted.

"Yes. Azriel is my foster-brother. You can trust me."

"Oh, yes, yes!" She clung to my hand, and burst into tears of relief. "But—that? *That?*"

She was staring at the Golem.

"It is here to save you. It broke down the wall. Don't fear it; it is of God."

Yet she trembled, her great eyes fixed in anxiety but controlled by faith in my words.

"Golem," I now told it, "take us back to the ghetto."

But the Golem did not stir!

My heart fell. I knew I had to give positive, definite orders. But I did not see at first what was wrong. That broad, unmoving face of humanized clay could tell me nothing; the Golem could do nothing but what I commanded.

I looked desperately around—and then I realized how stupid *I* was. The slaughtered pig, the stoppered jar, the stone bottles, and a small parchment with writing on it . . . there was a purpose revealed in all this.

Taking the stopper out of the jar, I looked in— and closed it up again. A dreadful smell of blood came from it; it was in fact half-filled. I picked up the bottles and saw that each had a label.

I examined them separately.

My heart froze, then beat hard with rage. The largest read, "To be filled with the pig's blood and hidden in the ark of the Alt-Neu Synagogue."

The Ark! The Holy of Holies! To be "found" there by Batislav's men!

The next: "To be filled with the pig's blood and left in the house of the High Rabbi."

The third: "To be filled with the pig's blood and left in the Pincus Synagogue, in the women's balcony."

The fourth: "To be filled with the pig's blood and left in the house of the Shammas Avrahm."

Now it was all so clear.

They would arrive during the Seder, break in on the feast, and "find" the bottles. They would declare that this was the blood of the "murdered" Maria-Agnes— Christian blood, for secret use in our holy ceremonies.

I saw then that all this must go back with us to the ghetto.

What else? I looked about more carefully now.

In the shadows at the back of the pallet, there stood

a small, heavy-looking trunk of metal, a foot high and about two feet by one-and-a-half across; it was old and heavily rusted. I pulled it forward, and then saw that it was marked with brass nailheads, and that these nailheads, deeply sunken in, spelled out the words, S. A. N. T. A. M. A. D. R. E. It was strongly padlocked, but with a new, unrusted lock.

I tugged at it, but it was so heavy that I could barely lift it. I decided to leave it there for the time.

Everything else I gathered together in my arms: the jar, the bottles, and the slaughtered pig that still bled slightly. Maria-Agnes shut her eyes and shuddered at the sight of it. The note I stuffed into my shirt; it was in a language I did not know.

Quaking within, I again commanded the Golem.

"Take us back now to the ghetto."

The Golem moved. First it struck out of my arms everything that I was carrying! Then it picked me up and set me across its great, moist, rocky shoulders. Then it lifted Maria-Agnes, who stifled a cry as it put her under its left arm; then it picked up the pig's corpse; the stoppered jar and the bottles fitted into its huge right hand.

Then it turned, and began the long march back.

This time it seemed that whatever had willed the Golem's invisibility had put us all beyond human perception, for although it was now early afternoon, not one of the people we passed so swiftly seemed to be aware of either the Golem or what it carried.

Every moment of the long journey homeward prickled in my heart. It seemed to me that the Golem was taking a much longer path than before, that it did not move as fast, that it paused often, that it encountered difficulties, once—oh terror—that it might even have lost the way! Could it again leap the river? Was its triple load too heavy even for the strength of the Golem?

But then the High Rabbi's words came back to me: "Did I not bid you to fear nothing?" and my spirit calmed down.

Yet I anxiously watched the sky; it was early spring, and the days were not long. This evening would be the first night of Passover. It seemed to me that the first star was already trembling through the distant cloud. This meant that we were perilously close to the moment when the Seder would begin. Indeed, it was almost customary for observant Jews not to wait for all three stars to appear, but to hasten the formal arrival of the evening that began a holy day ("for the evening and the morning were the first day").

The first star came out.

Already the Golem approached the winding, gleaming line which was the River Ultava, behind which lay the ghetto of Prague. The outlines of the soaring Old Tyn Cathedral; the lofty statue of good King Wenceslas mounted on his prancing horse; the great sculpture of the battling giants, Good defeating Evil, before the Hradstyn Palace—all appeared in turn, darkening against the pale sky. In the spring fragrance of lilacs and jasmine from the terraced gardens of the hills of Prague, I suddenly thought of Leah. At last I saw the broad blue sparkle of the Ultava.

The Golem crossed the river in one leap. It was over the Karlsbridge, and now it strode through the city streets, but above the people.

The second star had come out.

But not yet the third.

Here was the gate of the ghetto, and the lamp before it still unlighted, and the Judengasse, and the Alt-Neu Synagogue, at last. The crowd, massed in the broad place: on one side the stern, troubled Jews, pressing defensively close to each other; on the other side, the mingled group of strangers, led by such men as we had seen there on the night of the Great Shabbat, when Count Batislav had made his cunning charge of the ritual murder of his daughter.

And there—how I thanked God—dominating with his powerful eyes the whole scene, on the steps of the synagogue, our High Rabbi Judah Loewe himself!

There the Golem, going to one side, still unseen, set down Maria-Agnes, then the pig's corpse, the jar, the bottles, and myself. I saw Azriel standing not far from the High Rabbi. Together with Maria-Agnes, I ran stealthily into the synagogue and sent for Azriel. While he and Maria-Agnes fell into each other's arms, I returned and gave the parchment note directly into the hand of the High Rabbi.

He read it and gazed in horror at the corpse of the pig. I showed him the jar and the bottles, and put them at his feet without a word. He understood instantly their import.

"Bring curtains from the wardrobe room," he ordered me, very quietly. "Cover all that—the pig and the jars. They will be our evidence, later, to the King. Tonight we must show only our joy, for God has delivered us. The King sent for me and would have given me a troop of soldiers. Thank God I refused it."

There were some who said that the third star did not come into the sky that night until some minutes past its time. This I do not know and cannot well agree with. But I know it did not come out nor did the sky grow entirely dark until the High Rabbi had spoken to the crowds.

When I returned to the synagogue steps and covered the pig's corpse and the jars, all was different from before. The Golem was still invisible to all but me and, I believe, to the High Rabbi. Radiant with relief and joy, the High Rabbi was gazing toward the wide-opened doors of the synagogue behind him.

A woman was coming out, smiling, and by the hand she led a shy small female now wrapped in a beautiful flowing white shawl. They stood together in front of the excited murmuring crowd.

In a loud, firm voice, the High Rabbi spoke:

"People of Prague, here I show you this maiden. Maiden, tell them your name."

"I am Maria-Agnes. Maria-Agnes von Lehn von Batislav."

"Whom do you believe to be your father?"

"My father—the Count Batislav."

"Has anyone here ill-used you?"

"No. Oh, no."

What a roar of joy went up! Joy, that is, from the Jews and those of the crowd who were friendly and believed in us, but of astonishment and perhaps disappointment from the hangers-on of Batislav and outsiders who had been hoping for a different kind of excitement.

So the High Rabbi turned and led us all into the synagogue.

Never was there such a feast of rejoicing and thankfulness to God as our celebration that evening of the first Seder of the Passover.

We all forgot, in the great excitement, about the Golem.

13

I woke at dawn with a shock.

I had forgotten the High Rabbi's orders.

How could I have forgotten? How could I have dared to forget?

The High Rabbi had trusted me—only because he had been compelled to leave for the royal castle of King Rudolf—and I had accepted the trust.

True, I had fulfilled the first part, that of guiding the Golem to find and bring back Maria-Agnes. Therefore, no doubt, the High Rabbi had felt that I could be depended upon to complete the task. I had been present at the creation of the Golem. It was proper that I should be the one to bring its imitation-life to its destined end.

Trembling with haste, anxious to do the work I had undertaken, I managed to throw on my clothes and to run to the gates of the Alt-Neu Synagogue before anyone else was fully up. The streets were almost empty; everyone was enjoying the happy sleep that follows relief from the fearful tension that we had suffered for many days.

Before the gates the Golem was still standing motionless, and visible only to me. None of the few persons who began to pass by showed awareness of this huge, grayish-red, man-shaped figure, patient as a statue in front of the synagogue.

As I came closer, I saw—and a strange sadness came over me—that it was pleased at my coming.

"Golem," I exclaimed, hastily, "go down now to your place in the cellar of the house of the High Rabbi."

The great creature obediently turned and marched in front of me, and I followed it to the house.

We went inside and down the steps.

Now it stood, silent, in the dim cellar.

Its pale eyes dwelled on me, so patiently, so trustingly. Surely that was a look—almost, I would have said, a look of contentment, perhaps even of pride, that it had done well.

It seemed almost to be waiting for a word of praise, of approval. And I felt such words coming to my lips; it had done us all urgent service.

But this was absurd; I knew it. After all, it was not

a soul. It was mere animated clay. Had I not myself been one of those who compiled the earth of which it was made?

And it had grown. It was now almost twelve feet tall! Surely it had grown by the natural fertility of earth, as a tree grows, but much faster because of the spark of directly God-given life within the clay. But this was only another reason why it must be returned to clay. For its strength was enormous. Its face had almost human appearance. It moved less stiffly.

Who could say how far it might go toward becoming human? And with its rate of growth, if it should become less innocent, it could become dangerous, unmanageable. And not having a reasoning mind, what harm it might do!

Firmly I began to utter the mystic command of the High Rabbi.

"Golem," I intoned, clearly and solemnly, yet now knowing there was a pain at my heart because of such apparent cruel injustice to one who had saved us from injustice, "in the name of the Eternal Power which gave thee life, return—"

Before I could utter the last fatal words, to my astonishment a flash of fear startled in the pale eyes high above me.

The great arm slowly raised itself in a pleading gesture.

From that huge mouth came a pitiful wail, thin and helpless as a baby's cry.

I was stunned to see that the Golem knew it must cease to exist, and that it did not want to end.

And how was it different in this from us who were human souls? Were not we also brought into this life without our willing it, without knowing our purpose and our fate?

Had this being done wrong?

No. Less than we. It had served us, obeyed us, demanding nothing, only that it might continue to exist. Why was I beginning to feel that it might also love, and hope, and fear?

No. I could not destroy him.

I knew I was wrong—I must be wrong—to disobey the High Rabbi. But I would go back, I would beg the High Rabbi to release me from this task which I was too weak to fulfill. Someone else must do it.

I turned to go. . . . But I was too late.

As if released by the turning away of my eyes which had held it in the spell of the command to give up its spirit, the Golem broke out of the cellar and strode past me!

Wildly and at a tremendous pace it rushed out into the street.

It had become visible!

And it had totally changed!

Now it raised its huge arms. It broke and crashed everything it passed. It uprooted trees that had withstood a hundred years of storm and gale. It pulled out horses from their carts and carriages and flung them miles away! It split houses and threw their parts into the wind. It crushed people under its feet.

Everything living ran madly from it.

Soon it circled!

It was coming back to the house of the High Rabbi!

As it turned, I saw it. Alas, how fearful that face was now! Its eyes were red with tears. Its big lips poured slaver and slime. It made horrible short cries. It glared blindly upon all.

Already the High Rabbi was rushing out of his house, holding up his staff that was beginning to flash and gleam. His eyes were wild with horror and anguish; his lips were muttering rapidly.

Now he was running down the steps, close to the little tree rooted in its dark blue and light blue tiles.

Suddenly a flare of pink dress came flying down after him. Young Leah was racing ahead of her grandfather, her hands out as if to protect him, hurrying before him to meet the Golem in its fury—as if she could stop that raging onrush!

The figure of the High Rabbi seemed to tower to twice his height, his long staff stretched out straight, his voice thundering with superhuman force strange

Everything living ran madly from it.

words, the staff now flashing violent rings of fire and brilliant sparks toward the Golem, and then the High Rabbi's charge:

"Golem, in the name of the Eternal power which gave thee life, return thy spirit to whence it came!"

The Golem stopped. It writhed frightfully.

But Leah, crying out in terror, had run ahead of the High Rabbi; the Golem had lifted its stony arm—the arm was about to fall upon her—and I rushed in between.

I felt as though I had been sheared in two.

I saw the Golem crash down in a heap of charred clay before the outstretched staff of the High Rabbi.

Then I fell. I saw blackness. Then nothing.

Yet even as I fell into darkness, I was certain that the Golem had not meant to do anything evil; that it had behaved more like a terrified animal, mad with fear, that did not know its own strength and did not know what it was doing.

And the fault was mine. For who knew better than I that the command to end the Golem's existence had come to the High Rabbi directly from God? That its continued life would be a fatal error in destiny? And I had not followed the High Rabbi's command; I had not trusted it; I had thought that I was wiser.

14

The fist of the Golem would surely have crushed either Leah or me into dust, if it had been swung intentionally. But my injury was the result of a huge mass collapsing close to me, and the weight struck only a glancing blow. Even in its end, the Golem had meant us no harm.

For many, many days and nights, as I was later told, I was barely alive. The left side of my head, which had suffered the hammerlike impact, performed its share of the perpetual miracle God creates in our bodies by which we cure ourselves without knowing how. The bones were brought together, the flesh healed, the skin grew back, and at last there were only a few scars remaining on my cheek.

To me it seemed that there was nothing in the world but the walls of my room. I knew only that I breathed and that I saw. There was neither day nor night, and no person but Leah. Doctors came and went. Sometimes I dreamed. I dreamed of the High Rabbi, praised be his name, that he stood beside me, a gentle smile of understanding kindness on his lips; I saw that he uttered prayers, and then I felt a deep, still refreshment of my spirit.

Without being able at the time to measure the meaning of what he said to the men who came in with him—these must have been Yitzak Kohen, Leah's father, Avrahm, my foster-father, and Jakob Sasson, all were his disciples and friends—I sensed that he had prayed to God to spare my life and not to destroy my soul. Wherefore he believed that I was to live, but that my disobedience had incurred discipline. The arrogance through which I had followed my own weak judgment instead of obeying the holy command must be wiped out by my never coming back to the normal powers of my mind; my brain would remain at the level of a small child, for as long as my natural life.

Furthermore, I must not be allowed to enter the peace of the future life until the exile of the Jewish people should be ended. I must learn that to put away death is to misunderstand the purpose of life.

Which of this was dream? Which happened indeed?
Sometimes I dreamed I saw my good foster-father Avrahm ben Hayim, but at first I could not remember who he was. He wept. I could not tell why, for all seemed happy and restful as I lay there.

Then there came two, a young man with noble dark eyes and a gentle girl of beauty. They kept telling me their names were Azriel and Miriam-Anna. I knew them, I saw them, but I did not know why they came to me—but her face was happy and young as the sky at dawn! And she smiled at Azriel holding her ringed hand.

And then sometimes—often—I dreamed of my poor Mutterli. She did not touch me, as the others did, stroking me or patting me. She wore a soft light around her head, and she would say, gently, "Give me your prayers," or "Give me your blessing," and her face would shine upon me, and she smiled.

But always there was my Leah, my lovely, my blessed one. And then, one day, when I was able again to stand and then to walk, though still as if in dream, she came to me in the white robe of an angel, it seemed to me, from among many other people. She came with the High Rabbi, and there were prayers and tears—only Leah smiled—and then the others went away, but Leah stayed with me. My Leah had married me. There had been no special ceremony, except for the marriage vows. Her tutor, Saul of Wurms, had chosen a different bride, and Leah never spoke of him any more.

And I was happy; yes, I was always happy after that. If there were sorrows, if there were troubles, I never heard about them. Perhaps I was told, but I did not understand, and I could not tell why other people frowned or wept, when all was so peaceful and fair.

Often we walked in the fields around the city, we saw the blue sky, the blossoming of flowers, and children ran up to play with me.

Sometimes the little ones hung back and seemed afraid. Afraid—of *me*! But Leah had a special charm for that; she would put her pretty hand up to her forehead, and shake her head, and smile, and then it seemed they understood her, and that would make them come up to me.

Sometimes we would all sit on the grass, and they would sing, and sometimes the song was about Gideon ben Israyel. Then sometimes the little girls would run up and kiss me. I would feel sure that I knew him, but at that time I did not realize that he and I were the same person!

At first, when they would ask me to tell them about the Golem, I could recall nothing. But more and more it would come back to me. I would tell them what I remembered, and they would be struck with wonder!

Now and then a boy would say, "Psha! I don't believe it!" Then the other boys would jump on him, and they would have a fight—but a friendly one, a friendly one.

Ah, it is endless years since all these have gone and that I have remained here alone, with my task of watching over the charred heap of clay that was once the Golem. It lies here still, covered up with the remains of many ancient Hebrew manuscripts and books. For it is a custom of the Jews never to destroy anything that might have the name of God written upon it. But even those parchments inscribed in my own time have become worn and spotted, here in this attic of the Pincus Synagogue.

Yet I wait in peace, even in contentment, for it will come—that day when the Lord will turn back the captivity of His people, the gates of Jerusalem shall be rebuilt. I shall be free to die, and my Leah will know it and she will come for me.

בָּרוּךְ אַתָּה ה׳ דַּיַּן הָאֱמֶת׃

Blessed art Thou, O Lord, the righteous Judge

Note

It was reported that Maria-Agnes proved to be not the daughter of the evil Count Batislav. She was the child of a Spanish-Jewish family, who had been living in Spain as secret Jews (Maranos) while forced by the Inquisition to pretend to be converted. They were emigrating on the *Santa Madre* to Amsterdam, where there was a strong and free Jewish community. The ship had been seized by pirates, who looted and then sank it. The parents drowned; the child, Miriam-Anna, was saved to be sold as part of the booty. Count Batislav, who was involved in backing the piracy, received her. He adopted her in the expectation of some day making legal claim to the box of gold pieces which her family had brought with them, and also of becoming a partial heir to their estates in Spain.

He had let years go by, in order to cloud her childhood recollections of the wreck, and to scatter other possible witnesses to the facts. Then he decided he could use the girl to free himself of his large debts to the ghetto community of Prague. This resulted, however, in the discovery of her real origin.

F   I   N   I   S

Format by Gloria Bressler
Set in 12 point Granjon
Composed by Haddon Craftsmen
Printed by Neff Lithographers
Bound by Haddon Craftsmen
HARPER & ROW, PUBLISHERS, INCORPORATED

About the Author

Sulamith Ish-Kishor was born in London. Later she settled with her family in New York City, where she studied history and languages at Hunter College. A published writer since childhood, Miss Ish-Kishor has contributed articles and fiction to many distinguished magazines. Her books include A BOY OF OLD PRAGUE, THE CARPET OF SOLOMON, OUR EDDIE (runner-up for the 1970 Newbery Medal), and DRUSILLA: A NOVEL OF THE EMPEROR HADRIAN.

About the Artist

Arnold Lobel was born in Los Angeles and grew up in Schenectady, New York. FROG AND TOAD ARE FRIENDS, which he wrote as well as illustrated, was runner-up for the 1971 Caldecott Medal and the 1971 National Book Award for Children's Literature. Mr. Lobel was graduated from Pratt Institute and lives in Brooklyn, New York, with his wife Anita (also a writer and illustrator of children's books) and their two children, Adrianne and Adam.